THE TWELVE DAYS OF CHRISTMAS

Illustrated by Claire Counihan

SCHOLASTIC INC.

New York   Toronto   London   Auckland   Sydney

About the Illustrations

All the illustrations in this book are photographs of cakes and cookies baked and decorated by the artist specifically for *The Twelve Days of Christmas*. The background of each picture is a cake covered with colored icing. The actual Christmas gifts are represented by gingerbread cookies. Gumdrops, marzipan, jelly beans, candy canes, and other candies form the trees, flowers, floors, and borders of each illustration.

ISBN 0-590-42918-3

12 11 10 9 8 7 6 5 4   2 3/9

Printed in the U.S.A.   23

First Scholastic printing, October 1989

for Eva
and Nancy

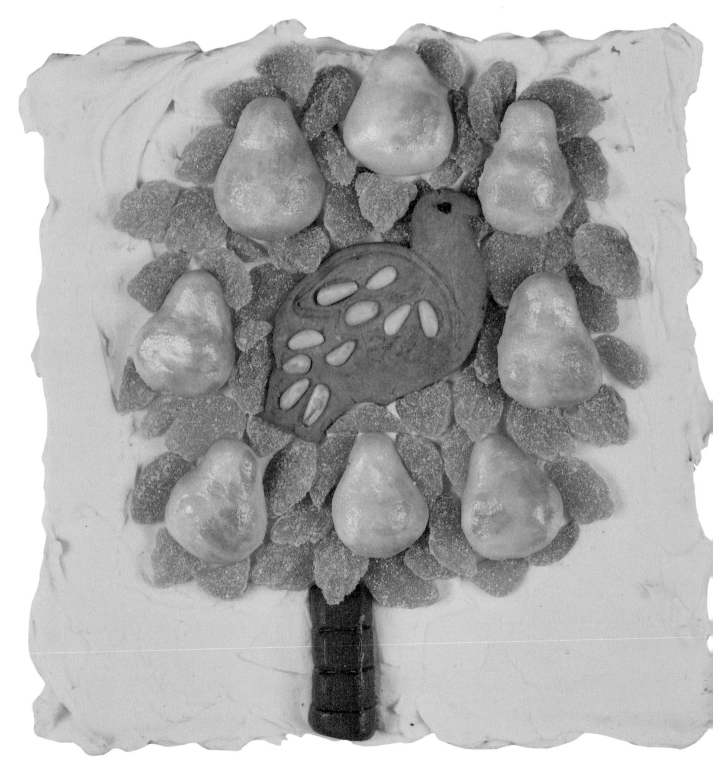

ON the first day of Christmas
my true love gave to me
a partridge in a pear tree.

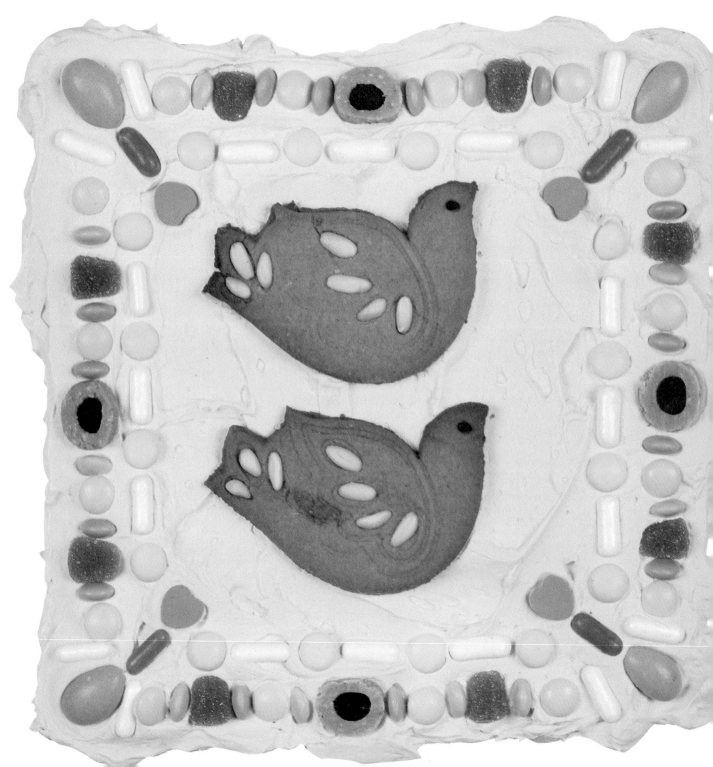

On the second day of Christmas
my true love gave to me
two turtledoves,
and a partridge in a pear tree.

On the third day of Christmas
my true love gave to me
three French hens,
two turtledoves,
and a partridge in a pear tree.

On the fourth day of Christmas
my true love gave to me
four calling birds,
three French hens,
two turtledoves,
and a partridge in a pear tree.

On the fifth day of Christmas
my true love gave to me
five golden rings,
four calling birds,
three French hens,
two turtledoves,
and a partridge in a pear tree.

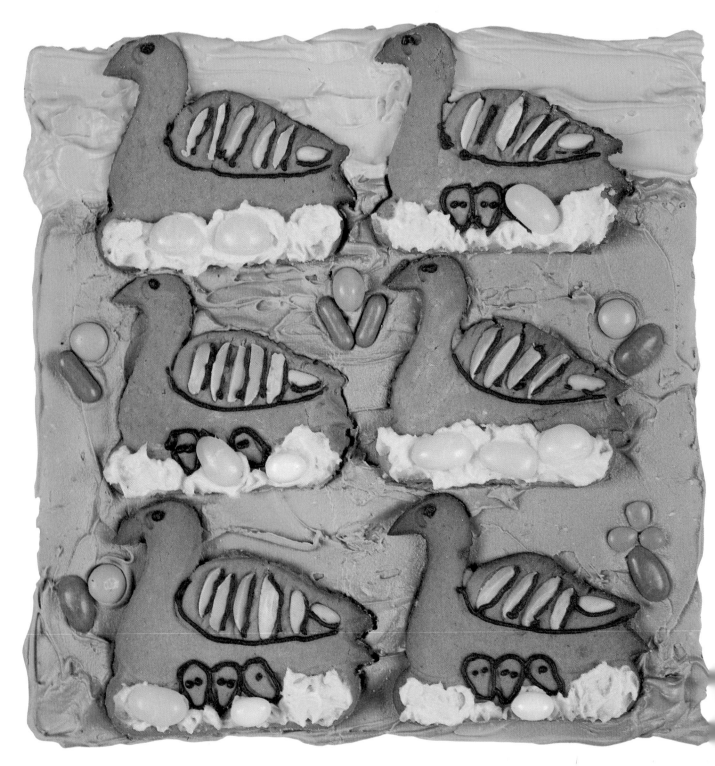

On the sixth day of Christmas
my true love gave to me
six geese a-laying,
five golden rings,
four calling birds,
three French hens,
two turtledoves,
and a partridge in a pear tree.

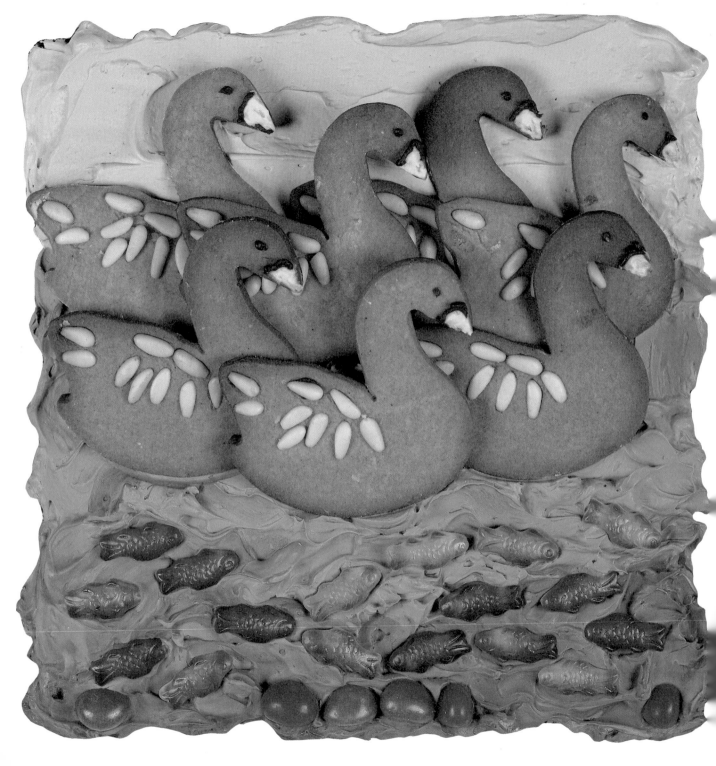

On the seventh day of Christmas
my true love gave to me
seven swans a-swimming,
six geese a-laying,
five golden rings,
four calling birds,
three French hens,
two turtledoves,
and a partridge in a pear tree.

On the eighth day of Christmas
my true love gave to me
eight maids a-milking,
seven swans a-swimming,
six geese a-laying,
five golden rings,
four calling birds,
three French hens,
two turtledoves,
and a partridge in a pear tree.

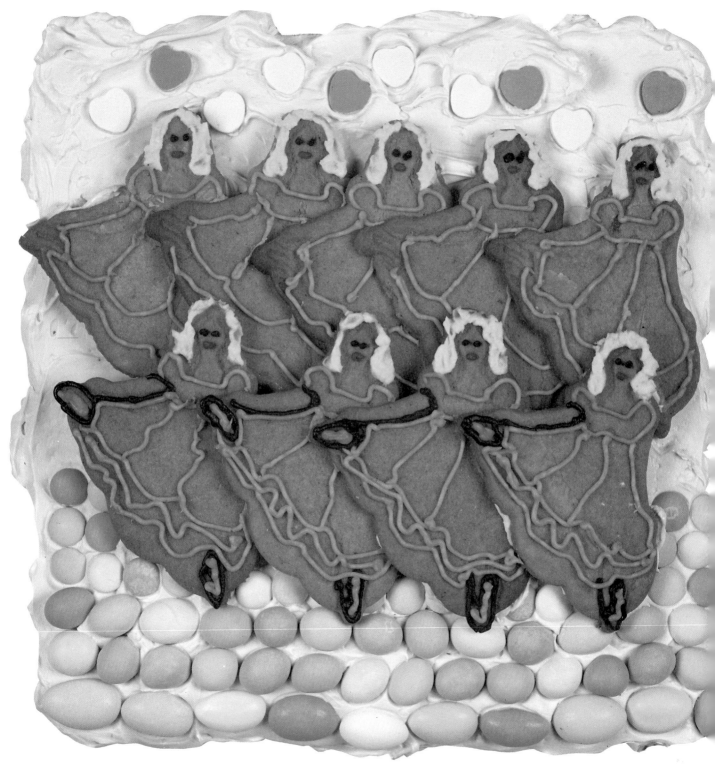

On the ninth day of Christmas
my true love gave to me
nine ladies dancing,
eight maids a-milking,
seven swans a-swimming,
six geese a-laying,
five golden rings,
four calling birds,
three French hens,
two turtledoves,
and a partridge in a pear tree.

On the tenth day of Christmas
my true love gave to me
ten lords a-leaping,
nine ladies dancing,
eight maids a-milking,
seven swans a-swimming,
six geese a-laying,
five golden rings,
four calling birds,
three French hens,
two turtledoves,
and a partridge in a pear tree.

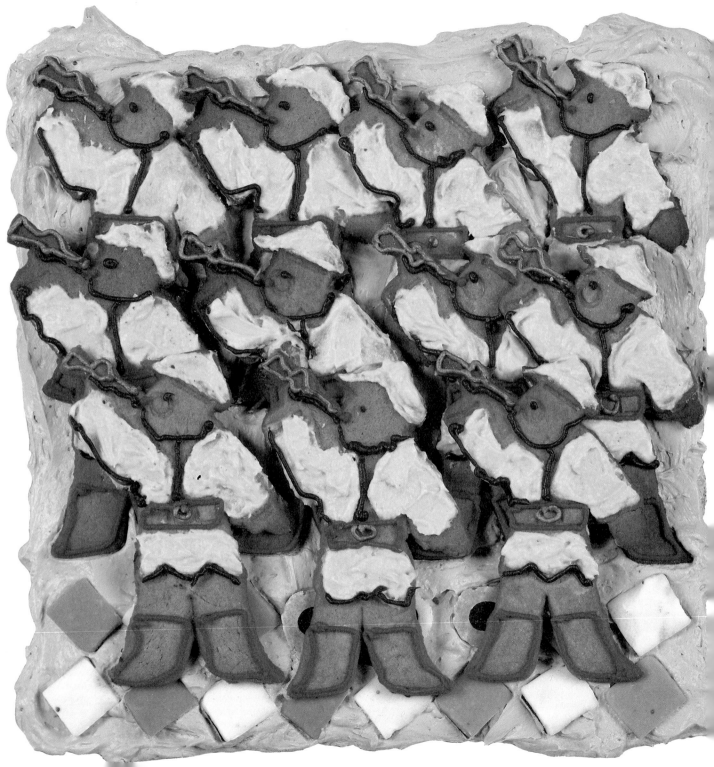

On the eleventh day of Christmas
my true love gave to me
eleven pipers piping,
ten lords a-leaping,
nine ladies dancing,
eight maids a-milking,
seven swans a-swimming,
six geese a-laying,
five golden rings,
four calling birds,
three French hens,
two turtledoves,
and a partridge in a pear tree.

On the twelfth day of Christmas
my true love gave to me
twelve drummers drumming,
eleven pipers piping,
ten lords a-leaping,
nine ladies dancing,
eight maids a-milking,
seven swans a-swimming,
six geese a-laying,
five golden rings,
four calling birds,
three French hens,
two turtledoves,
and a partridge in a pear tree.

The Twelve Days of Christmas

par - tridge   in a   pear   tree.   6. On   the   sixth
7. On   the   sev-enth
8. On   the   eighth
9. On   the   ninth   day of   Christ - mas   my
10. On   the   tenth
11. On   the   elev-enth
12. On   the   twelfth

true   love   gave   to   me: Six   geese a - lay - ing,
Sev-en   swans a - swim-ming,
Eight   maids a - milk - ing,
Nine   la - dies   dancing,
Ten   lords a - leaping,
Elev-en   pip - ers   pip - ing,
Twelve   drum-mers   drum-ming,

five   golden   rings,   four   calling   birds, three   French   hens,

two   tur-tle   doves,   And   a   par - tridge   in   a   pear   tree.

You can make gingerbread cookies
just like the ones in this book.
Ask a grown-up to help you.

You will need:

1 cup butter or margarine,
    softened
1 cup light brown sugar
½ cup honey
3½ cups flour, sifted

2 teaspoons ginger
1 teaspoon cinnamon
1 teaspoon baking soda
a dash of salt

1 tablespoon butter or margarine to grease the cookie sheet

You will also need:

electric mixer   cookie cutters   spatula
rolling pin   cookie sheet

Optional ingredients:

raisins   walnuts   cake icing

Here's what you do:

1. Put all the ingredients, except the extra tablespoon of margarine or butter, the raisins, the nuts, and the icing, in a large mixing bowl.

2. Use an electric mixer on medium speed. Mix the ingredients until they are well combined.

3. Chill the dough in the refrigerator for one hour.

4. After you have taken the dough out of the refrigerator, preheat your oven to 350 degrees.

5. Put the dough on a board that is lightly covered with flour.

6. Use a rolling pin to roll out the dough until it is ⅛ of an inch thick.

7. Use a cookie cutter to cut the dough into shapes.

8. Grease your cookie sheet with the extra tablespoon of margarine or butter.

9. Use a spatula to move your gingerbread cookies onto the greased cookie sheet.

10. Decorate your cookies with the raisins and walnuts.

11. Bake the cookies for 8–10 minutes.

12. When the cookies have cooled, decorate them with cake icing.

The Story of Gingerbread

THE history of gingerbread begins almost two thousand years ago, when the ancient Romans brought a spice called ginger to Europe from India. Europeans loved the taste and smell of the brown spice. But it wasn't until hundreds of years later that they learned to mix the ginger with bread crumbs, honey, and other spices to make the first gingerbread cookies.

Gingerbread was especially popular in England. When the English people came to America, they brought gingerbread recipes with them. Some American bakers baked gingerbread alphabets. When children learned their letters, they were allowed to eat them! Martha Washington baked gingerbread cookies for her husband, George Washington. Years later, President Abraham Lincoln said, "I don't suppose anybody on earth likes gingerbread better than I do."

In the 1800s, Americans started to hang gingerbread ornaments on their Christmas trees. They decorated their trees with gingerbread hearts, stars, goats, houses, and men. It didn't take long for baking gingerbread to become a Christmas tradition in families all over America. It's a tradition many families keep even to this day.